Treehouse,
Stories for Boys

Basketball, School, Friends
Stories that changed my life

by John Chipley

Gotham Books

30 N Gould St.
Ste. 20820, Sheridan, WY 82801
https://gothambooksinc.com/

Phone: 1 (307) 464-7800

© 2025 *John Chipley*. All rights reserved.

No part of this book may be reproduced, stored in a retrieval system, or transmitted by any means without the written permission of the author.

Published by Gotham Books (May 31, 2025)

ISBN: 979-8-3493-8553-7 (P)
ISBN: 979-8-3493-8554-4 (E)

Because of the dynamic nature of the Internet, any web addresses or links contained in this book may have changed since publication and may no longer be valid.

The views expressed in this work are solely those of the author and do not necessarily reflect the views of the publisher, and the publisher hereby disclaims any responsibility for them.

Contents

Introduction iv
Story #1: Making friends 1
Story #2: Momma 6
Story #3: The three boys 11
Story #4: My dog George 16
Story #5: Buddy 21
Story #6: Finding George 24
Story #7: Pastor Moore and the dog pit 28
Story #8: The Dog Pit 31
Story #9: Saying Goodbye 36
Story #10: What about Buddy 41
Story #11: Waldo 45
Story #12: The Secret 50
Story #13: Where is Waldo? 53
Story #14: School 58
Story #15: Learning can be fun! 61
Story #16: They Broke My Leg 64
Story #17: The Pink Shoes 67
Story #18: The Gift of Mudita 74
Story #19: The Kiss 79
Story #20: A boy named Alec 84
Story #21: Goodnight Papa 87
Postscript 88

Introduction

When I was eight, it wasn't easy being eight. I don't think I would have made it through school (or life) without Papa's love and all his crazy stories.

My name is Abraham, but everyone just calls me Little A. I'm African American, kind of short, skinny, and have awesome dreadlocks. Life is suddenly beginning to get interesting. It's called growing up.

This book is full of stories, my Papa's stories. These are stories that were told to me by my grandfather, Papa. Papa was a funny old man. He

Treehouse, Stories for Boys

was short and very round. He didn't have any hair and wore round wire rim glasses. He loved to laugh and swore that all his stories were true. I believed him, but you can judge for yourself.

After Grandma died, Papa moved in with our family. We had a small house, so Papa and I shared a bedroom, **MY** bedroom.

I know this sounds crazy, but Papa, sometimes, acted more like he was my age than his. He was eighty-one and had a million stories. Every night, before going to sleep, I always asked Papa to tell me a story about when he was my age. His stories fascinated me. They made me laugh, made me cry, and, if he had a little glass of whiskey before coming to bed, sometimes his stories embarrassed me.

Papa once told me about the treehouse he built when he was my age. He told me it was built on the top limbs of a very tall tree. Did your grandfather ever build a tree house, a tall treehouse? Well, mine did, and he told me he used to pee out the back window.

Yes, he was a funny old man. And when he moved in with us, Papa and I built a tree house in my back yard. And, yes, one day I peed out the back window, but I lost my balance and fell out of the window. I broke my arm. Papa thought it was funny. I didn't. I was embarrassed. When people came running over to help me, my pants were down around my knees. **NOT GOOD!**

Papa grew up in the enter-city of Memphis, Tennessee. His neighborhood was known for crime and bad people. It wasn't a place most people would want to live, but it was Papa's home.

Papa's birth name was Abraham, but when he was about my age everyone started calling him Abe. I was named after Papa. So, when I was born, everyone started calling me Little A.

Papa didn't grow up in a family like mine.

He grew up with an old lady he called Momma, but it wasn't his real mom. No one ever knew who Momma really was. According to Papa, she was his grandmother. She was very smart. I think, maybe, she was a little too smart. You will understand after reading a few stories.

Papa and Momma were very poor, but Papa told me that Momma never told him they were poor. So, he never knew they were poor. However, he did know one thing. He knew they lived in a neighborhood full of danger. It was the type of neighborhood where everyone went inside when the sun went down.

Like I said earlier, Papa was a great storyteller. He told me stories about everything. He talked about basketball, Momma, his friends, his dog, his school, a horse named Henry, a cow named Nancy, a white boy named Peter, and even what I called just plain crazy stories. I have written down as many stories as I can remember. They take up the pages of more than one book. I will keep writing. This is just book #1. Book #2 will follow, and maybe even book #3.

Papa told me things that all boys need to know; things his Momma taught him. He also told me stories about a crazy old man called UT. You're going to love UT. He is in book #2, along with Nancy, Henry, Joshua, Betsy, and Peter.

You're going to love Nancy the cow, Henry the horse, Joshua, Betsy, and Peter. So, keep reading. Plus, I haven't even mentioned the Mountain People yet. They are also in book #2, or book #3. I must warn you; you're **not** going to like the mountain people.

I'm writing these stories because Papa died last year, and I'm not a little boy anymore. I am now twelve, almost a man.

I still miss Papa's stories at night. I am writing Papa's stories down so one day my children might enjoy reading them. Or maybe one day I will read them to my grandchildren when they go to bed.

Papa was more than a grandfather. Papa was my best friend. Friends you make as a young boy are friends you never forget, NEVER! Maybe you have a grandfather or an uncle like my Papa. I sure hope you do.

Treehouse, Stories for Boys

I never want to forget Papa, and I never want to forget his stories. I hope you will enjoy the following stories just as much as I did when I was a young boy.

Story #1

Making friends

One night after getting in bed, I asked Papa if he ever played basketball when he was a boy. Had basketball even been invented back then? Papa laughed and looked over at me.

Papa's bed was on one side of the bedroom and my bed was on the other side. It was a small room, so our beds were close to each other. Papa sat up in his bed and started telling me his first story.

Papa's Story:

"Boy, I loved three things, basketball, Momma, and my dog, George. When I turned twelve years old, I was shorter than the other boys. However, I could dunk a basketball from almost anywhere outside or inside the three-point line. So, don't let anyone tell you that you are too short to play basketball.

"I was good, REAL1Y GOOD! However, this turned out to be both good and bad. I've seen boys in my old neighborhood get into fights over playing basketball. Little A, work hard to be your best at everything, but remember, as a boy, basketball is just a game. Play hard but have fun.

"You are lucky to live in a nice neighborhood. I never see you fighting with other children while playing ball. You're always laughing and having fun. That makes me feel good. Little A, growing up in my old neighborhood was not like your neighborhood. It was a daily fight for survival.

"In my old neighborhood, basketball was not a game. I grew up in a part of town that was known for having rough kids. Living in my neighborhood was NOT Mr. Roger's neighborhood. I quickly learned how to read other boys by the way they walked or by the way they swaggered. I noticed how they dressed, what colors they wore, what words they said, and even what their shoes looked like.

Treehouse, Stories for Boys

"You are a very lucky young boy. When I was your age, my life was determined by the big boys, especially one boy named Markus. Markus was big, **REAL big**. He was bad to the bone. He always stole my cokes while I was shooting baskets, ALWAYS. One day I told him to stop. He pushed me down and laughed at me. He called me a lot of bad names.

Little A, I was mad, but he was HUGE. So, I came up with an idea on how to get back at him, and it worked.

"Whenever I couldn't go poop, Momma would mix something in a glass and make me drink it. After drinking whatever was in the glass, I went poop and poop and more poop. So, I found the bottle Momma used on me and pored some of it into my coke can. That afternoon, I placed my coke on the bench and started shooting baskets. Markus came over, called me a bad name, and took my coke. He looked at me and yelled, **'Thanks, you little wimp'**.

"Little A, I watched Markus as he drank my coke. I shot baskets and waited for a reaction, and it didn't take long. Markus got this funny look on his face, and then he started moving back and forth on the bench. Then it happened. **HE EXPLODED!** Poop went everywhere. His pants turned dark brown, and he smelled like a garbage truck. And, best of all, he was sitting with his girlfriend when all this happened. Markus looked over at me and YELLED some more very bad words! I just waved at him and told him I would go get him another coke if he wanted one. Then I ran like a mad man back to the safety of my apartment.

Little A, sometimes big bullies just need a reminder that size isn't everything. I couldn't stop laughing all day long. However, when I told Momma what I did, she reminded me that it wasn't over yet. She told me that he would get back at me.

"Momma told me I had to make friends with Markus.

If I didn't, he just might have the last laugh. So, I went to the store and bought some flowers for his girlfriend, and I wrote a note telling her what a great guy Markus was, and I apologized.

"It worked! The girlfriend was happy, and Markus got credit for the flowers. I actually had a new friend. Strange how things work out sometimes.

"Momma was right, it's better to make friends then enemies. Momma was right about almost everything. I will tell you more about Momma tomorrow. She was amazing.

Now, however, it's time for me to end this story and get some sleep. Good night, young man.

Story # 2

Momma

One night before I fell asleep, I asked Papa what his Momma was like? Was she a good cook? Did she have a lot of rules? Papa looked over at me with a huge smile on his face. I could tell by the grin on his face this was going to be a great story.

Papa's Story:

"Little A, God comes in many forms, and I think Momma was one of those forms. You already know she wasn't my real mom. She found me at a laundromat, and at the time she was already an old lady. She lived off of a small social security check and food stamps.

"But she didn't hesitate to pick me up and take me home with her. I was in a cardboard box. Momma told me I was the size of a small dog and still pink. Inside the box next to me was an envelope full of all the necessary papers. So, Momma decided to keep me, at least for a few days.

"Well, those days soon became months, and the months became years. Momma figured that sooner or later someone would come knocking at her door looking for me, but no one ever did. So, Momma believed it was God's plan for her to take care of me. She had me baptized, and from that day on I was all hers.

"Momma was a special kind of lady. She was old, very old, when she found me. She didn't have any money, and she could hardly walk. But Momma was very religious. She believed that God sent me to her for a reason, and she wasn't about to say NO to God.

"She read the Bible every day. She read out loud so I could hear her reading. The words she read were full of wisdom and love and truth. Little A, I was fed words from the Bible long before I could read. Those words shaped who I was going to be when I grew up. They were the foundation of who I eventually became. Words feed the mind, just like food feeds the body. Momma knew that a strong body and weak mind was a dangerous combination. Momma worked hard at filling my mind full of knowledge. This knowledge started with the Word, but it also included other things boys needed to know. It included building my attitude and character."

I asked Papa, **"Papa what's attitude and character?"**

"Attitude and character, Little A, are what you are on the inside. It's your soul! It's who you are, not how you look. Your attitude is how you see things. Do you see the good in people or do you see the bad? Your character is what you do. Momma didn't know it, but she was my teacher as well as my mom. She didn't have a classroom with four walls full of pretty pictures, but she taught me with her words and her actions.

"Children, all children, learn by watching other people. They learn how to be bad, or they learn how to be good." Momma knew this and talked about it with me. She loved to tell me stories.

One of her stories, one that was my favorite, was about being an honest person; being a person full of good character. Momma told me that most people had a price on being good and honest. Then she told me a story that illustrated her point.

She told me the story of the three boys.

"Little A, I will have to save that story for tomorrow night. However, I want to tell you something funny about Momma. She always carried a snake, a very large snake, in her purse. It was a corn snake and harmless. However, it was large and looked deadly. At night it crawled around our apartment and took care of the rats. She named it Roscoe. It was her pet and lived in her very large red and fuzzy purse. She called her purse her healing purse. It had a large wooden cross glued to one side. Momma healed a lot of boys who tried to steal things from her (or anyone). I loved to watch as she would quietly tell a boy to put something back that he had just stolen. They would look at Momma, call her some rude names, and start to walk away.

Then Momma would open up her healing purse and pull-out Roscoe. She would just stand there holding Roscoe as the boy put whatever he had stolen back on the shelf. She would just smile and say, thank you.

"Now, Little A, let's get some sleep. I'll tell you about the three boys tomorrow. Good night my young friend."

Story # 3

The three boys

The next night I asked Papa to tell me Momma's story of the three boys. Papa told me that this story just might be her best and most important story.

Papa's Momma's story:

"Little A, once there was a boy, a boy just your age, who found a bag of money sitting on a park bench where someone had probably been waiting for a bus. Inside the bag were five one-dollar bills. Along with the money, this boy also found a card with a person's name and phone number. It was

just five dollars, but he wanted to do the right thing. So, he called the number. The man thanked the young boy and told him to just keep the money as a reward for his honesty.

"There was another boy who also found a bag of money sitting on a park bench where someone had been waiting for a bus. Inside this bag the boy found ten twenty-dollar bills. Along with the money he also found a note with a person's name and phone number. two-hundred dollars was a lot of money, and the person was stupid to leave it there. So, he decided to keep the money. He could buy a lot of video games with that much money.

But after getting home, he changed his mind. He called the phone number. The person who lost the money was overjoyed, thanked the boy, and picked up the bag of money at the boy's house. There was no reward, but the boy felt good about returning the money. He did the right thing.

"Then there was another boy who found a bag of money sitting on a park bench where someone had been waiting for a bus. Inside this bag was over five-thousand dollars. Along with the money, he found the name of a local company. Now this was a lot of money! But no one was around, so how would anyone know who picked it up. So, this boy took the money and buried it in his back yard.

"He waited a month before spending any of the money. He got away with it, he thought. Then he discovered what he did. The money was the payroll of a small company. The loss of the money caused the company to have to close its doors. Ten people lost their jobs. One of those people was this boy's best friend's dad. His best friend's family had to sell their house and move to an apartment in another part of town. This boy was too ashamed to tell anyone what he did. This one bad decision hurt him deep inside, and he never forgot what he did.

"This boy had to live with his decision for the rest of his life. He stopped spending the money. The money wasn't his. He thought about the harm he had done to so many people. And now, he couldn't undo what he did.

"The moral of this story, Little A, is to always make the right choice, **regardless of the cost**.

Remember, sometimes we can't undo bad decisions.

"Little A, what we do is important. It is called our **CHARACTER**. Your character is more important than any amount of money. And yes, sometimes it does come with a very high price.

"Sometimes it might make you feel very little. Sometimes it might cost you a friendship. If a friend of yours steals something, you need to get a new friend. That's hard to do, but we really

are judged by the people we hang with. It's true!

Be careful!

"Little A, your **attitude** is what you see. Do you see the good in people and yourself, or do you see the bad? When you make a mistake, do you learn a lesson, or do you blame someone else?

"Little A, life is a crazy game, like basketball. It's a game with lots of moves. Somewhere along the way you are going to do the wrong thing, or you might say the wrong thing. Unfortunate, but this is life. We all make mistakes! The person who wins the game is the one who is honest, learns from what they did, and always comes back up from making a mistake.

"You might miss a basket. You might lose the game. You might get caught cheating on a test. This is unfortunate, but it is also a test. It is a test of your character and your attitude. The ability to get back up and keep going when you do something stupid is the key to both ATTITUDE AND CHARACTER.

"Little A, it's past my bedtime. Tomorrow night, remind me to tell you about my dog, George.

You're going to love George.

"Good night young man, good night."

Story # 4

My dog George

Tonight, Papa told me about his dog George, and it wasn't what I was expecting. It wasn't what I wanted to hear.

Papa's Story:

"Little A, life isn't fair, but it is what it is. This story is hard for me to talk about. George was twelve years old. We were the same age.

George was more like a brother than a dog. We went everywhere together, and he even slept on the foot of my bed every night. According to his registration papers from the shelter, George was part lab and part shepherd. To me, he was love on four legs.

"Momma said we were like two peas in a pod. Wherever you saw one, the other was always there. George went to school with me regardless of the weather, and he waited for me under the shelter of a large oak tree that stood next to the front door of the school. On rainy days the principal would let George sleep in his office.

"I think George could actually talk. I didn't understand what he was trying to say when he barked, but I know he understood my words. I never gave George commands or had him do stupid dog tricks. I just talked to George like I talk to you. The only difference was George was smarter than most of my friends. George spoke to me with his eyes, the tilt of his head, and the wagging of his tail. He also spoke to me with a very cold nose. His cold nose on my arm told me to pay attention. He seemed to know things that most people didn't know. Frankly, I think he could smell bad people and would push me away from them. It was like he could see inside someone. I think George thought I was another dog, not his owner or a person. And that was okay with me. However, life can be hard, and sometimes bad things happen to all of us, even George.

"When I woke up one Sunday morning, George wasn't

on the foot of my bed, and Momma was sitting on the edge of my bed. It was Sunday, and Momma should have been getting ready for church, not sitting on my bed. Her face was red from crying. She looked over at me and told me that last night some boys broke into our apartment and took George. George was gone! They left a note for me on the kitchen table. The note read, 'Stay out of our territory or we will kill George'.

"Momma told me she heard voices and George barking, then everything went silent. When she got to my room, George was gone. I yelled, **GONE? WHERE'S GEORGE? WHAT DO YOU MEAN GONE?**

"Momma called the police, but the gang didn't steal anything, like a TV. They just broke into our apartment and took George. They left a note telling me to stay out of their territory. Taking George was their way of punishing me.

"The police told me that the gang wouldn't kill George, but they would probably train him to be a fighting dog, a killing dog. I was also told that it would be almost impossible to find him. And if they did find George, he wouldn't be the same dog I had. Gangs were very good at retraining dogs from being good to being bad, very bad. The cops told me to just get another dog. They told me that George was gone, and there was nothing they could do. Then they handed me some papers and just walked away. I stood there as they told me to forget about George and just get another dog. I was mad, real mad!

"I yelled back at them, **GET ANOTHER DOG? GEORGE IS MY DOG! HE'S LIKE MY BROTHER! GET ANOTHER DOG? ARE YOU CRAZY? LISTEN TO ME! IF YOU WON'T TRY TO FIND GEORGE, I WILL! AND I WILL FIND HIM!**

"I ran back to my room, slammed the door, jumped on my bed, screamed, and cried. I cried until there were no more tears. The next morning came before I was ready for it to come. It wasn't like in the movies. When I woke up, George wasn't sitting next to my bed wagging his tail. NO!

George was still gone, and I was still alone.

"I sat on the edge of my bed just thinking about George. Where was he? What were they doing to him? And how would I go about finding him. The one thing I didn't think about was would George try to run away and find me?

"Now, it's late Little A. I'm tired. It's time for us to get some sleep. I'll tell you more about George tomorrow. O.K.? I promise."

Story # 5

Buddy

I could hardly wait to hear the rest of Papa's story. I was in bed early, waiting for Papa. I called out, "Hurry up Papa, hurry up!"

Papa's story:

"Little A, the next day one of the cops came back to our apartment, Officer Tom. He had a cute little puppy wrapped up in a police blanket. He handed the puppy to me. He told me his name was Buddy. Buddy was a new police dog in training. He needed a family for buddy to live with for the next few months. Buddy was just a puppy, but he needed to learn how to be both a family dog and a police force dog. Officer Tom needed me to help train Buddy. In a few months, he would pick up Buddy and start teaching him on how to be a police dog. He told me that I was the perfect trainer for Buddy and asked me to help. I admit, I didn't want to do it. However, I think George would have wanted me to do it. So, I agreed to help, but I told Officer Tom, when I find George, Buddy will have to find another home.

"Officer Tom agreed and handed Buddy over to me. As soon as I took Buddy, he suddenly leaped out of my arms, ran into my apartment, and jumped on the foot of my bed, (exactly where George always slept). I laughed and asked Officer Tom if he was sure Buddy was a police dog? Looked to me as if he just liked to sleep. Officer Tom laughed and told me that Buddy was a special breed of dog with an amazing ability to smell drugs. He told me that Buddy cost over three-thousand dollars.

"He told me to train Buddy just like I trained George. Only, don't take him to school with me unless I had a cage for him. It's good for him to be around people, but he's just a puppy.

"After Officer Tom left, Buddy and I just sat on my bed and stared at each other. Then Buddy leaned over and licked my face. This was the start of our journey down a path that was full of fun, laughter, and adventure. Buddy wasn't

George, but I could tell he was special, very special.

"Little A, it's bedtime. Tomorrow, I'll tell you what Buddy did. You won't believe it."

Story # 6

Finding George

Tonight, I asked Papa if they ever found George. Papa sat up in bed and looked over at me. He looked sad. He just sat there for a long time not saying anything. Then he began to slowly tell me the rest of George's story. He told me what he didn't want to tell me.

Papa's story:

"Little A, one day when I got home from school, Buddy was sleeping on the foot of my bed with George's blanket in his mouth. I quickly grabbed some dog treats and sat next to him. I gave him a treat and praised him. I wanted Buddy to associate George's scent with a reward.

"I immediately called Officer Tom and told him what I did. Officer Tom yelled, **BINGO! THAT'S IT LITTLE A. BUDDY CAN HELP US FIND GEORGE!** Buddy has already learned George's scent, and he also associates George's scent with a reward.

"Officer Tom told me that I might have just solved our problem. Plus, I had also helped train Buddy to be a police dog.

"Officer Tom told me that tomorrow, after school, he was going to come over and take Buddy and me for a walk. Officer Tom told me that we were going to walk every day after school with Buddy. When we get home, we will give Buddy George's blanket and a treat. He told me that in just one week Buddy should be able to memorize and connect the scent and the treat. Then all we had to do was find someone with that same scent. Buddy would help us find George and, maybe, the dog pit. Much to Officer Tom's surprise, it all happened very fast.

"The very next day when Officer Tom came by to take Buddy (and me) for a walk, Pastor Moore was visiting Momma. I put Buddy's leash on him, and we started to walk out the front door. Just as we walked pass Momma and Pastor Moore, Buddy stopped. I gave Buddy a little pull and told him to follow me. He just sat there. I should have known what he was trying to tell me, but I didn't.

"After several pulls, Buddy walked out the front door and down the sidewalk. When we came to Pastor Moore's car, once again, Buddy suddenly stopped. He walked over to Pastor Moore's car and sat next to the front door. Then he looked over at me as if he wanted a treat for doing something good. Officer Tom told me that Buddy had already picked up on the scent we were looking for.

"He told me to stay with Buddy while he went to his car and got his GPS tracker. He soon returned and placed the tracker up under the pastor's car. Now he was able to follow Pastor Moore's car wherever it went. He gave Buddy another treat, and we continued our walk around the block and back to my apartment. I took Buddy and went inside. Officer Tom got in his car and turned on his GPS tracker. Now all we had to do was wait for Pastor Moore to take us to the next dog fight and hopefully find George.

"Little A, I'm tired. I've got to stop for tonight. I'll tell you the rest of the story tomorrow night, O.K.?"

Story #7

Pastor Moore and the dog pit

A week passed, and once again it was Saturday night. I didn't want to go to church the next morning. I asked Papa, when he was a boy, if he had to go to church every Sunday.

Papa's story:

"Yes sir. Little A, Momma always took me to church with her every Sunday. The church was just two blocks down the road from our apartment, but it took Momma a long time to walk just two blocks. We would start our walk right after breakfast and get to church around eleven o'clock. Momma never missed church or Pastor Moore's sermons on sin.

"Every Sunday Pastor Moore preached on sin. Sometimes he would get so excited he would call out people by name. No one ever got mad, and I thought it was funny. Momma sat in church and listen to every word Pastor Moore preached about sin.

"I would sit in church and think about ways to find George. I thought about George and prayed about him all the time. Momma listened to Pastor Moore's sermons and leaned on every word he said.

"One day on the way home from church, Momma asked me questions about the sermon. I was only twelve, but Momma worried about me and sin. Frankly, when it came to sin, I didn't trust Pastor Moore. He looked phony to me. He seemed to love the ladies of our church a little too much. All the kids could see it. He always complemented the old ladies on their hats and ate their food.

"My friend, Tyrone, told me there was no way Pastor Moore could afford to drive a big black Cadillac on his small salary, unless he had another income. Tyrone also told me that Pastor Moore was doing a lot more than just praying with the women of the church.

"Tyrone's dad was a deacon of the church and knew a lot about church thing. Tyrone would sit quietly and listen to his mom and dad talk about Pastor Moore. They thought it was funny. His parents said that Pastor Moore was a good man, but maybe a little more than just the hands and feet of God to some of the ladies. Then his parents would laugh. Tyrone was older than me and told me everything about Pastor Moore, sin, and sex.

"And yes, Little A, Momma did have Pastor Moore over for lunch every now and then. And, yes, when he came over, I always went outside to play and allowed them time to pray. Yes, the Lord does work in mysterious ways. However, Pastor Moore turned out to be a lot more mysterious than anyone knew. Little A, do you understand what I'm saying?"

"Yeah, Papa, I'm twelve. I know all about those things."

"Good, then let's get some sleep. Good night, boy."

Story # 8

The Dog Pit

Once again, I was in bed early. I told Papa to hurry up. I wanted to know what happened to George and Pastor Moore. Did they catch him? Was George, Okay?

Papa's story:

"Little A, officer Tom called me the next day and told me that Pastor Moore didn't go anywhere all day long, so we had to wait for him to make a move. He told me that when Pastor Moore started to move, he would call me. He told me to be ready to move in a hurry. Officer Tom said that he would have police cars ready to join us, but he wanted me to be there when and if they were able to rescue George.

"He told me that once the raid started, the gang members might try to harm George. So, everything had to happen like clockwork. He also told me that things will probably start to happen late at night, so I had to be ready to jump out of bed like a fireman. Officer Tom told me to keep my phone with me all night. If I got a call, I had to run to the street as fast as possible. He would be waiting for me.

"However, I couldn't sleep. I kept waiting for the phone to ring. Buddy seemed to know what was going on. He couldn't sleep either. Slowly he moved from the foot of my bed, up next to my head.

"It was around one o'clock in the morning when the phone rang. I quickly answered it. It was Officer Tom. He yelled at me to hurry. He was parked outside. I had to move fast!

"I jumped out of bed, tossed on some clothes, and ran out the front door. I saw Officer Tom's car. He flashed his lights, and I jumped into the front seat next to him. We took off at full speed. I could see three police cars behind us.

Officer Tom told me to buckle up and hang on. I watched the speedometer as the car moved faster and faster.

"The police cars following us turned on their blue lights, but no sirens. We were getting closer and closer to Paster Moore's car and, hopefully, to where the dog fights were taking place. As we turned the next corner, I could see a parking lot full of cars, along with the pastor's car. The building in front of all the cars was an abandoned warehouse. Suddenly, all the blue lights were turned off. We slowly and quietly pulled into the parking lot. No one said a word. Everyone talked with their hands.

"Officer Tom told me to stay in the car and wait for George. He commanded me to not leave the car! All the cops were out of their cars and ready to move. Then, SUDDENLY, the police busted through the warehouse door and ordered everyone to FREEZE. All I could hear was the sound of dogs barking.

Just then Officer Tom saw George and yelled for George **to come, COME! GEORGE, COME!**

"George came running toward Officer Tom at full speed. He hit him so hard it knocked him off his feet and the gun out of his hand. One of the gang members ran over to where Officer Tom was lying on the floor. He pulled out his gun and aimed it at Officer Tom. George leaped out of Officer Tom's arms and charged toward the man. Instantly, the man turned his gun toward George. He took aim and fired. Officer Tom tried to grab the man, but it was too late. Everything happened too fast.

"George fell to the floor, then he slowly crawled toward the open door. I could see George from the car and George saw me. His eyes were fixed on me as he made his way over to the car. I placed my head next to his. We just looked at each other.

Then his eyes slowly closed.

"Officer Tom came over and checked George. He was dead. Officer Tom held me while I cried.

"Little A, George was gone, and this time there was nothing I could do. Little A, sometimes this is the way life is. Sometimes there is nothing we can do but cry.

"Tomorrow, I will tell you the rest of the story. Tonight, I'm too tired. Little A, it's been a long time. I still miss old George.

"Good night. Good night young man. Good night, George."

Story # 9

Saying Goodbye

I told Papa I was sorry about George, but, after all the years, Papa was still very sad. If you have ever had a dog as your best friend, you know how Papa felt.

Papa's story:

"Little A, last night I told you a sad story. Some stories are sad. Sometimes life is sad, and the next morning wasn't any easier.

"When I woke up, Buddy was lying next to my head, not at my feet. And, to my surprise, Officer Tom was sleeping on the floor next to my bed. Momma came into my room with some coffee for Officer Tom and some hot coco for me. No one said a word at first. We were all tired and just trying to wake up. We all just sat there in silence. I don't think anyone knew what to say. Then I said the first words to Officer Tom, "what do we do now?"

"Little A, Officer Tom looked over at me and told me that George was a hero. He jumped between me and the man who was going to kill me.

"Officer Tom told me that George knew what he was doing. George saved Officer Tom. So, Officer Tom got permission for George to be buried in the police dog cemetery. This was a great honor.

Plus, the school principal had agreed to allow any student who wanted to attend the funeral time off from school. Officer Tom had made arrangements for George's funeral to be the next day.

"Then I asked Officer Tom about the men at the dog fight. What happened to them? He told me they all went to jail. Plus, they would all stay in jail until their trial."

Then I asked, "What about Pastor Moore? Did he also go to jail?"

"No! Little A, he didn't. You see, it wasn't Pastor Moore in the car. It was a man who picked up his car and washed it every week. Pastor Moore just paid the man to clean his car because the man needed money. He had no idea what the man was doing besides washing his car. I'm sure glad Officer Tom didn't arrest the wrong person.

"After Officer Tom left, I rolled over and went back to sleep. Buddy crawled up on my back and also went to sleep. From that day on Buddy never slept at the foot of my bed. He always slept next to me or on top of me. Our relationship was changing. On that day, just feeling his warm body against mine was better than any words anyone could have said.

"Buddy was now my dog, and I think Officer Tom knew it. I was supposed to give Buddy back to Officer Tom at the end of the month, but I knew that wasn't going to happen. Buddy was now mine and I was Buddy's.

"The next morning was George's funeral. Officer Tom pulled up in front of my apartment. This time he was in a real police car, blue lights and all. When I got in the front seat, Officer Tom told me that I was going to be surprised today. He just drove past my school and saw all the students getting on school buses.

"I just sat there and smiled. For the first time in a long time, I could smile. At times we all need other people. This was one of those times. Just then, three police motorcycles pulled up behind us and in front of us. Everyone turned on their blue lights. Officer Tom also flipped on his blue lights and we all slowly drove down the road toward the pet cemetery. All the traffic stopped for us as we drove through town and out to where George was waiting for me.

"As we approached the cemetery, all I could see was a long line of school buses and lots of kids. As we turned into the cemetery, all the kids waved at me. Officer Tom stopped his car. A policeman opened my door and walked with me over to where George was buried. Pastor Moore and Momma were already standing next to the grave. It was so quiet I could hear my heart pounding.

Pastor Moore said a few words and then all the kids started to applaud.

"I fell to my knees and began to cry. All I could do was cry. I was both sad and happy. The more I cried the better I felt. It's hard for me to describe. Little A, one day you will cry like I cried. Then you will understand.

"But tonight, young man, we will not cry. Tonight, we will enjoy being with each other. Good night my young man, good night."

Story # 10

What about Buddy

One night I asked Papa to go back and tell me about Buddy. What happened to Buddy? You didn't finish that story.

Papa's story:

"Well, Little A, after George's funeral, Buddy just settled in with me. However, remember Buddy was given to me to train as a family dog. Officer Tom told me that he would pick Buddy up after a month or so and then start Buddy's police dog training. However, a lot can happen in just one month, and a lot did happen!

"By the end of one month Buddy and I were inseparable. I understood that Buddy was in training to be a police dog, and not my dog. The problem was no one told Buddy about the plan.

After one month Buddy was bonded to me and I was bonded to him.

"Then, one Saturday morning, Officer Tom came by for a visit. It was time for Buddy to move to the police station and start his police dog training.

"Little A, I knew one day Officer Tom would come to get Buddy, but I still wasn't ready. Officer Tom asked me to come outside and talk with him, away from the ears of Buddy.

"Once we were outside, I told Officer Tom that I didn't want to give up Buddy. I begged Officer Tom to let me keep Buddy, but it didn't work.

Buddy had to leave with Officer Tom. Officer Tom told Me to go inside and get Buddy. He told me to bring Buddy outside and put him in the back seat of his car, then turn and just walk away.

"Little A, I just stood on the front porch and didn't move. Then Officer Tom told me that either I did it, or He would do it. I looked over at Officer Tom. Once again, I begged him to let me keep Buddy.

"Officer Tom Was a kind man. He reached over and hugged me. Tears were filling his eyes. He told me that he was sorry. He knew this would be hard for me, but Buddy is a police dog. He said I could visit Buddy anytime I wanted to, but I had to let Buddy be Buddy. I had to love him enough to let him go, but I couldn't do it.

"I wiped tears out of my eyes and yelled that it wasn't fair. **Buddy was my dog!** Officer Tom just stood there. He didn't say a word. He just looked down at me. I turned and went inside. In a few minutes I returned with Buddy. I opened the back door of Officer Tom's car and told Buddy to get in. Then I shut the door, turned, and walked back to my apartment. I was both mad and sad. All I could do was stand on the front porch and watch as Officer Tom got in his car and started driving off.

"Little A, I stood there and watched as Buddy looked out the rear window of the car at me. Suddenly Buddy started barking. It was a different kind of bark. Buddy was trying to tell us something. As the car approached the end of the block, I could hear Buddy barking over and over and over.

"At the end of the block the car stopped. It just sat there not moving for a long time. Then, I watched as Officer Tom stepped out of the car, looked over at me, and opened the back door.

"Buddy leaped out of the car and ran at full speed back to me. Officer Tom just stood next to his car and watched. He waved goodbye, got back into his car, and drove off without Buddy.

"Little A, Buddy sat next to me on the porch steps, and we watched as Officer Tom's car disappeared out of sight. We just sat there staring at each other. Then Buddy gave me a big wet lick on my face, and I started laughing.

"**Little A, sometimes life isn't fair, and sometimes it is! Good night young man.**"

Story # 11

Waldo

I told Papa about a student in school who always picked on me. I asked him what I should do. The boy was a lot bigger than me.

Papa's story:

"Every day in school was a new day. Some of the big kids always tried to make my life miserable. Almost every day there was a fight in one of the restrooms. School at times felt more like a war zone, but I was lucky. I had a friend named Waldo. Waldo was BIG! Waldo could hurt you if he wanted to.

"Waldo seemed to hate everyone but me. He liked me because I helped him with his homework. He was close to failing, and my teacher asked me if I would help him with his lessons. I agreed, and in return he agreed to help protect me. He even joined me on my bathroom breaks. When he was with me no one picked on me.

"As I said, Waldo could hurt you if he wanted to. One day, when Waldo was just a freshman, a senior boy told him to move out of his way. Waldo grabbed the boy, picked him up off the floor, and tossed him down the stairs. That was all it took. After that, no one messed with Waldo, NO ONE!

And, because Waldo and I always sat together at lunch, no one bothered me.

"Waldo was actually a nice guy and very funny. At first, I didn't know why he didn't like people. Then, one day at lunch, it stumbled out of his mouth. I discovered that Waldo was homeless. He was homeless and no one knew it! No one, that is, except the school janitor.

"I couldn't believe his story. He told me that he woke up one morning, about a year ago, and his apartment was empty. His mom and new stepdad were gone. Waldo said he looked around the house for his mom and found a note on the kitchen table.

The note told him that he was on his own.

"His parents were gone, and they didn't tell him where they were going. The note told him to live in the apartment as long as possible. Waldo told me that he sold everything in the apartment to his neighbors and then just walked away. He didn't want anyone to know that he was homeless and told me not to tell anyone. If the school system found out that he was homeless, they would put him in a group home.

"I asked Waldo where he slept at night, where did he got his food, and take a shower. He told me that the janitor at our school saw him on a street corner one night. The janitor knew he was homeless without Waldo having to tell him. So, the janitor made a copy of the school key for Waldo. They worked together on a plan for Waldo to sleep at the school, eat leftovers, and shower in the gym. Waldo said that the janitor had been protecting him all this time. No one, so far, had caught him living at the school. When Waldo told me his story it made my blood run cold.

"Then he told me that no one missed him, no one cares about him, no one loved him, NO ONE. Then he told me he didn't hate people, he only hated himself. He said that I was the only person he talked to every day.

"When Waldo said that I almost choked on my food. I told Waldo that I was his friend. I cared about him and told him to never forget it.

"Waldo just sat there. He didn't say another word. When we finished lunch, we each got up and went our separate ways to class. I couldn't get Waldo's words out of my head.

"Little A, it was just too crazy. I knew I had to do something to help him, but what? I gave him my word that I wouldn't tell anyone, but I still had to help him. So, I went to Momma. She was the only person I knew I could trust. If I did the wrong thing, Waldo would run away and hide someplace else. And this time Waldo would never be found.

Treehouse, Stories for Boys

"Little A, it's getting late. I'm tired. I'll tell you the rest of the story tomorrow. Goodnight young man."

Story #12

The Secret

I was in bed early. I couldn't wait to hear what Papa did. Was Waldo okay, or did he run away and hide?

Papa's story:

"Little A, when I told Momma about Waldo, she couldn't believe it was true. She thought I was joking, but I wasn't. When she realized I wasn't joking, she placed her hands over her mouth to conceal her emotions. Then she told me, Abraham, you need to bring him home. He needs to feel safe with us. We can be his family.

"Little A, there was no way Momma was going to let Waldo live by himself. However, Momma didn't know the whole story. Waldo had been hurt by many people; even his own mom walked away from him. He

no longer understood the word Love. He no longer understood what it was like to feel safe. At this point in his life all he could feel was survival. He no longer trusted anyone.

"I told Momma I would talk with Waldo. Maybe he would change his mind and come home with me.

However, I did what Waldo told me NOT to do, I told someone else. So, I never told him that I talked to Momma. Living at the school seemed to be working. So, I decided that it would be better for me to join him, than for him to join me.

However, I wasn't sure of anything. Maybe, in trying to help Waldo, I would cause him more harm. I didn't know what to do. So, once again, I talked with Momma. What she said surprised me and scared me.

"She told me that Waldo was like a wild animal. A life that sounds strange to us just might be comfortable to him. If I tried to change his way of living, he just might lash out at me. This is what animals do. Only if he trusts me would he come to me. Then she asked me if I thought he trusted me, or was he just testing me?

"Little A, Momma caught me off guard. I had to think about what she said for a while. Finally, I told Momma that I though he trusted me. If he told me about living at the school and how he was abandoned by his mom, he must trust me.

"Momma just looked over at me, but she didn't say a word. She just tilted her head downward and gave me that look. Little A, she gave me a look that said be careful, be very careful.

"Little A, it's time to turn off the lights. You've got school tomorrow. Good night young man. I'll tell you more about Waldo tomorrow."

Story # 13

Where is Waldo?

Papa had just crawled into bed when he heard me ask, "Papa, what did you tell Waldo?"

Papa's Story:

"Well, Little A, I didn't tell Waldo anything. I was afraid he would run. However, I called Pastor Moore. I asked him if we could talk. He told me to come over to the church. He was working on his Sunday sermon, but he would much rather go fishing and talk with me. I didn't tell him that I had never been fishing before, I don't think it mattered. We just needed a quiet place where we could talk.

"Soon, Paster Moore and I were at a lake fishing, talking, and laughing. After about an hour of small talk, Pastor Moore looked over at me and asked me if I was ever going to tell him why I was there, or did I need more time. He told me that he loved fishing, but he thought there was something I wanted to ask me or tell me.

"Little A, there was a long pause. I pulled in my line and sat on the ground next to the pond that didn't have any fish, (at least not for us).

Pastor Moore also pulled in his line. Then, once again, I did what I told Waldo I wouldn't do. I told Pastor Moore the story about Waldo. I had to find help for Waldo before someone else found him and caused him to run away. Pastor Moore told me he had an idea.

"He was getting too old to keep the church running by myself and could use some help. So, he would print up a church bulletin, just one, for me to show Waldo. In this one bulletin he would advertise for a young person to help him around the church. If Waldo answered the ad, he would get the job and a place to live. I told Pastor Moore that that was lying. Pastor Moore just looked at me and replied, **what would Jesus do?**

"The next day Pastor Moore printed up a special bulletin for me to give to Waldo. At lunch the next day I showed Waldo the bulletin. On the back side of the bulletin was the following ad.

(Young person needed to help around the church after school and on weekends. Please call Pastor Moore at 223-0242 if interested.)

"When I showed the bulletin to Waldo, He didn't look excited. However, that afternoon he went to visit Pastor Moore, (and, of course, he got the job and a place to live).

"After Waldo moved into the church, his personality began to change. Little A, I didn't know exactly how to talk about this change with Waldo. Then, one day at lunch, I just told him what I saw.

"At first, Waldo began to laugh. Then, suddenly, he stopped laughing. His face looked different, like he was going to be sick or something. Then he laid his head on the table and told me he wasn't the same person.

"He told me that he had been talking with Pastor Moore, and something happened. He told me that he was not the person he used to be. Then he quietly started to cry.

"I have never heard anyone cry with such emotion or feeling. He was crying and trying to talk at the same time. His entire body was shaking. By this time everyone had left the cafeteria. It was just the two of us. Then the school principal came over to where we were sitting.

"She asked me if Waldo was okay. Waldo lifted his head up off the table. He looked at me, then he looked over at the principal, then back at me.

Then he told me he was cleaning the church and found a bulletin someone had left behind. It was the same bulletin I had given him, only this bulletin didn't have an ad on the back page. So, Waldo went to the files where Pastor Moore kept his bulletins. He found several copies of the same bulletin, and all were without the ad.

"He asked Pastor Moore about the ad, and Pastor Moore told Waldo what I did and why. At first, Waldo said he was mad. I promised Waldo that I wouldn't tell anyone. Then he realized what I did and why I did it. Waldo realized that I really did care about him, and so did Pastor Moore. And so did so many people who brought food to him and Pastor Moore. Little A, Waldo had people who cared about him. Waldo now had a family of people who loved him.

"Little A, love changes people, and God is love. When people try to tell you who or what God is, just remember Waldo. Now say your prayers. Good night young man."

Story # 14

School

One night I asked Papa if school was hard for him. I told Papa that I had lots of homework every night. I asked Papa if he liked school? Was it hard for him? Did he also have lots of homework? Did he make good grades?

Papa's Story:

"Papa looked over at me. Little A, you know I was a teacher. What you don't know is, when I was your age, I wasn't a good student. I wasn't real smart. I had to work hard for my grades. Little A, no one is born smart. We all have to work for our grades. However, everyone is different, and every brain is different. Some students do catch on to things quicker than others. My brain was not like that.

"When I was your age, I loved only three things: basketball, Momma, and my dog, George. I didn't liked school. However, I did like my fourth-grade teacher, Mr. Ford. He changed my life. I never told him that. I wish I had! He needed to know.

"Little A, if you ever have a special teacher, please tell them they are special. They need to know. They need to hear you say it.

"When it came to school, Momma told me that anything of value took time and hard work, especially grades. She told me that smart kids who do not study become dumb kids. She also told me that getting into college came before getting into the NBA. So, my grades were more important than making baskets. The pro teams only scouted college players. And good grades were the key to getting into college.

"If I wanted to be in the NBA, I first had to make good grades. So, that is what I did. It wasn't easy for me, but I knew I was as smart as anyone else. I also knew that the more I studied, the better my grades would be. Anyone can make good grades, but it takes time and hard work. No one is born smart, NO ONE! It requires work, just like being a good basketball player requires work. Practice really does make perfect. It is the only way.

"Little A, our skin color may be white or brown or purple, but our brains are all the same color. However, we all learn in different ways. There is no right way or wrong way. There is only **YOUR** way, and Mr. Ford helped me find my way.

"But tonight, Little A, it's getting late, and I'm tired. Tomorrow, I'll tell you how to improve your grades and have fun doing it. But I've got to stop for tonight."

Story #15

Learning can be fun!

Papa, I hate spelling. I try, but I always forget the rules. Were you a good speller? Mom wants me to be in the school spelling bee next week. Papa, I don't have a chance.

Papa's story:

"Little A, you are not going to believe this story. However, I swear it's true. When I was your age, basketball was how I learned to spell. All the boys in my school loved to play basketball during recess.

"One day while we were playing basketball, our teacher, Mr. Ford, realized that basketball could be a great tool for teaching us almost any subject. It all started while we were shooting baskets in a game of horse. Mr. Ford stopped the game and told us that, starting tomorrow, our baskets only counted if we could spell one of our spelling words for that week. That totally changed the game. We didn't understand. It sounded like Mr. Ford was taking the fun out of recess. However, we were wrong.

"The next day in class he announced that he was going to give us TWO HOURS of recess, not just one. That got everyone's attention! Then he told us the new recess game plan, and we all loved it.

"He told our class to study our weekly spelling words. Starting on Monday, we would play a game of horse for one hour. Everyone would have a chance to make a basket. When they made a basket, he would call out a spelling word for them to spell. If they could spell the word correctly, the basket counted. Every student would get three words to spell. If they spelled all three words correctly, they wouldn't have to take the Friday spelling test, and they would receive a grade of 'A'.

"**SPELLING SUDDENLY BECAME FUN!** And this was just the beginning of how Mr. Ford started using basketball, dodge ball, and even jump rope as a teaching tool. It sounds crazy, but it worked. We were having fun and learning at the same time.

Plus, there was always a Friday test for any student who failed during recess. Most students asked to take the Friday test. It gave them extra points.

"Mr. Ford also had a trick for teaching reading, grammar, science, and history. Plus, every week, he asked every student to write a story about themselves. Just one page. This was a story just for him to read. We were allowed to say how we felt, and it helped me to get through some hard times. Mr. Ford was special. Once again, learning was fun. Plus, at the end of the school year, Mr. Ford gave every student their collection of stories that they had written over the school year. SCHOOL WAS FUN! And I still have my stories, stories I wrote when I was your age.

"Little A, tomorrow, ask your teacher if she would let you play basketball and take a spelling test at the same time. See what she says. Good luck, and good night young man."

Story # 16

They Broke My Leg

I asked Papa if he ever got into a fight when he was at school? Mom told me to NEVER fight. But today at school a boy hit me for no reason, and I hit him back. Now I'm in big trouble.

Papa's story:

"Little A, it's hard to walk away when someone hits you. I know, I've been there. Little A, **YOU HAVE TO DO IT!** Sorry, but you were wrong to hit another student.

"School was fun for me. However, one day the same thing happened to me. The school down the road from our school challenged us to a basketball tournament. The other school was a private school. Everyone at that school wore uniforms and arrived at school in fancy cars. They also had a large gym and a basketball coach.

"My school was small and poor. We didn't have a gym. We practiced outside using an old basketball court with cracked concrete as our floor. We didn't have uniforms or a coach. So, it seemed as if everyone was betting on the private school to win.

"Little A, I was short, but I was still the team's best player. I was also like the team's coach. Our team was pretty good, but then the unthinkable happened.

"One day, while I was leaving school, a boy came over and hit me for no reason. Just like you, I hit him back. When I did that, things began to change in a hurry. I found myself surrounded by a gang of boys, boys that I didn't recognize. And they all had baseball bats. It was too late for me to run. All I could do was wait.

"They started hitting me with their bats until everyone heard a loud cracking sound. It was my right leg. They broke my leg.

"Little A, I fell to the ground as the gang of boys ran away. That was when I heard their voices. They sounded different from any of the gang members in my neighborhood. Plus, all they wanted to do was hurt me. They didn't want to take anything. They didn't yell warnings at me. These boys were not from my school. So, who were they? And why did they break my leg?

"My leg was put in a soft cast, and I was sent home from the hospital. I was told to stay off my leg for five weeks. This meant I couldn't play in the basketball tournament. This also meant that our school was probably not going to win the game. Now I knew why they broke my leg.

"They were from the other school and had money riding on the game. They wanted to make sure that their school won.

"Little A, I know what it's like to get in a fight at school, but your mom is right. I learned the hard way. However, tomorrow I will tell you the rest of the story. Now, let's get some sleep."

Story #17

The Pink Shoes

Once again, I was in bed early. Just as soon as Papa got in bed, I sat up and asked, "Papa, what happened? What did you do?"

Papa's story:

"Little A, the big game was just one week away. All I could do was sit on the bench and watch as our team practiced, and it wasn't pretty.

"Then one day, out of nowhere, this girl walked over and sat on the bench next to me. She said her name was Kujja. I had never seen her before, and I knew everyone in the neighborhood. I asked her where she lived. She told me that wasn't important. She just wanted to watch our team practice. That was when I noticed that she was wearing a school uniform. I asked her if she was from the school down the street. She replied, yep.

"Little A, I asked her if she was here to spy on us. Again, she just smiled and told me, yep.

I asked her if that was fair? She told me, nope.

"She was funny. I laughed and told her if it's not fair she shouldn't be here.

"Little A, her answer was crazy. She told me that she was there to help my team win. She told me she knew the boys who broke my leg. They have a lot of money riding on the game, and wanted to make sure their school won, not mine. And you are the player they felt that needed to be eliminated from the game.

"Little A, I didn't understand. The damage was done. They broke my leg. However, I told Kujja

that I thought we could still win.

"Kujja just shook her head and told me there was no way. Their school coach had been watching our team practice for a long time. They know every play and every player. Without me, she said our team didn't have a chance.

"Little A, I just sat there and didn't say a word for a long time. I was both mad and confused. I asked Kujja why she was telling me all this stuff?'

"She just smiled and told me she wanted to make it a fair game. She said, 'I'm here to put you back in the game.'

"I started laughing. I told Kujja that unless God came down and healed me, I didn't think that was going to happen. Kujja told me that she knew that my grandmother took me to church every Sunday.

She asked me if I believed in the power of God?

"I had to think about that question for a few minutes. I was a believer, but I didn't think God had time for basketball. Then I started laughing.

"However, Kujja didn't laugh. She told me I was wrong. She told me God loves basketball. Why do you think I'm here? God won't fix the game, but

He sure can fix your leg.

"Little A, I just sat there and stared at Kujja. I asked her how God was going to do that? Was He going to send down an angel to heal me?

"Kujja told me, maybe. She told me to just show up at the game, sit on the bench, and wait for her.

"Then she stood up, winked at me, and walked away. Little A, I didn't know what to believe, or who to believe. However, I did what Kujja told me to do.

"Soon it was game day. Our school team showed up for the game. It wasn't pretty. By half time, our team was losing by over twenty points. I just sat on the bench and watched as the other team kept scoring baskets. Little A, it was painful to watch.

"Then, during the half time, Kujja showed up and sat next to me on the bench. She whispered for me to swap shoes with her. I looked down. Kujja was wearing pink shoes. Kujja told me again to swap shoes with her. I looked down at her shoes. PINK! Again, Kujja told me, **'NOW! QUICK! DO IT NOW!'**

"Little A, I pulled off my shoes and pushed them with my foot over to Kujja. She then pushed her pink shoes over to me. **PINK!** I could feel everyone watching me, but it didn't matter. I picked up the pink shoes and put them on.

"As soon as I put on the shoes my leg stopped hurting. I reached down and felt my leg. It was healed.

"I slowly stood up and walked out onto the basketball court. I could feel everyone in the gym watched me as I walked around the court.

"Suddenly, everyone stopped talking. The silence in the gym was deafening. The only sound I could hear was the sound of my pink shoes rubbing against the hardwood floor.

"When the game continued, it was a new game. Everyone fed the ball to me. They don't care where I was standing on the court. I never missed a shot, NOT ONE! And I could slam dunk the ball just like the tall boys.

"Little A, I didn't know what was happening, but I loved every minute of it. Every person in the stands was on their feet cheering me on. What looked like a runaway game for the other school soon changed. It was now our school that had control of the game. It was a race against time. We were twenty points behind. We kept control of the ball the entire second half. When the final buzzer sounded, we were ahead by one point. We won!

"When the other team walked off the court, I sat down on the bench and handed the pink shoes back to Kujja. Kujja just winked at me and walked away. I walked home barefoot. And yes, my leg was healed. To this day I don't know how it all happened, but it did. Yes, Little A, God does love basketball!

"I never saw Kujja again after that day. And no one in the gym remembers ever seeing her. All they saw were the pink shoes, and now the shoes were gone, along with Kujja.

"Little A, you go to church. Do you believe in God, or do you just pretend to believe? I can't explain what happened, but I know what I saw. I know that God is always there, even at a basketball game.

"**Now say your prayers and get some sleep. Good night, boy.**"

Story #18

The Gift of Mudita

One-night I asked Papa why he wanted to be a teacher. It was a strange question, but school was hard for him. School is also hard for me.

Papa's story:

"Little A, you know I wasn't a very smart kid, but I always wanted to be a teacher, and I wanted to be a good teacher. I wanted to be the best! As a boy growing up, I had too many bad teachers. However, Dr. Ragland was a good teacher. I wanted to be a teacher just like her. I knew this would take a lot of work. I knew this would take a lot of time in both school and college. It would also take a lot of time outside of school. It would take time away from playing basketball all day with my friends. Little A, I still played basketball, but I always saved time for my schoolwork.

"Little A, I saw something too many boys never see. School was not a game. School was my ticket to a better future. It was my only way out, and I knew it. Some of my friends made fun of me. I tried to tell them what I saw, but they said I was crazy. They said I was a dreamer. Thank God I didn't listen to them. I still played ball, but I knew that my grades came first. Then I met Dr.

Ragland. She was my eighth-grade teacher.

"One day at school, after everyone else had gone home, I was helping Dr. Ragland clean her classroom. I told her that one day I was going to be a teacher. When I told Dr. Ragland that, she asked me to sit down and listen to her. I didn't know what to expect. I thought I was in trouble, but I sat down and waited.

"Dr. Ragland took her time before saying anything. When she started to talk, her voice was different. She didn't sound like a teacher; she sounded more like a parent.

"She smiled and said in a quiet voice that there wasn't anything more important than being a teacher, a good teacher. she told me that she never married. She never had children. She told me that her students were her children. Once again there was a long pause. Then she continued.

"She told me if I was serious about being a teacher she would help me. Teachers don't make a lot of money, but she had saved some money out of every paycheck to pay for her children's education. However, she never married or had any children. She told me if I still wanted to be a teacher after finishing high school, she would help pay my way to college.

"She only asked one thing from me. She asked that I only tell my momma and no one else. She said that I would make a great teacher and helping me would bring her great joy.

"Little A, I sat frozen at my desk. I couldn't believe what I just heard. I didn't know what to say. Thank you sounded so small. What do you say to a teacher who offers to pay for your college education?

"Little A, I stood up and slowly walked over to Dr. Ragland. She extended her hand in friendship. Little A, I shook her hand and then gave her a hug. I gave her a HUGE hug! Then I turned and started walking out of her classroom.

"Then I heard her said, "MUDITA, Little A, MUDITA."

I stopped. I turned and asked her what Mudita meant. She told me it meant that she got joy from my joy. She wrote the word on a piece of paper and handed it to me. Little A, I still have that piece of paper!

"Walking home was like walking on a cloud. I now knew that I really was going to be a teacher. It felt more like a reality than a dream. I had been through some bad days, but this was a good day.

This was the best day of my life!

"Halfway home I started running. I ran the rest of the way home. I could hardly wait to tell Momma. I ran into the kitchen and shouted, Momma, Momma, Momma, you're not going to believe what just happened. Momma, I'm going to college!

"Little A, you bring me a lot of joy. Love Ya, boy. Now, let's get some sleep. MUDITA!"

Story # 19

The Kiss

One night I was working on my list of spelling words while Papa was getting ready for bed. I was saying each word out loud, and then I would spell the word. Papa put off going to bed, came over, and helped me with my words. Then he told me a story about a spelling bee he was in when he was my age.

Papa's story:

"Little A, one day a new girl joined our class. Her name was Bralyn. She was from Africa. Her family had just moved to America.

"Bralyn was different from other girls. Bralyn could play a mean game of one-on-one basketball. Plus, she could outrun any boy in our school. She was taller than most boys, and her skinny frame was pure muscle. She had long tight dark brown brads and strong legs that that were both long and fast. She told me that when she lived in Africa, she would try to outrun the trains that went through her small village.

"She was very fast and could outrun most trains. The passengers would cheer her on and toss her coins as a reward.

"She only wore shoes at school, any other time she always went barefoot. Bralyn's desk sat right in front of mine. She was very pretty, and, yes, I was in love.

"Little A, this was my first love, my first girlfriend; and I didn't know how to tell her (or anybody). So, I just kept it to myself.

"Bralyn was smart and well educated. This is what made our relationship interesting. Bralyn didn't like being second at anything, and I was the same way. In just a few weeks it was time for the annual school spelling bee, and we both were determined to win.

"I went to the library and checked out several books on spelling words for the seventh and eighth grade level. I worked with Momma on as many words as possible. I also knew how to sound out words that I didn't know. I thought I was ready. I knew I was going to win, but when the day of the contest came, it was close, too close.

"Bralyn, it turned out, was good at everything, especially spelling. The competition started off with thirty students. After one hour it was down to just two, Bralyn and me. We went back and forth for over one hour. Then Bralyn was asked to spell the word "Heirloom".

"She stood quietly for a long time, sounding out the word in her head. Then she said, "Heirloom, H-E-I-R-L-O-O-M." She spelled the word correctly, and everyone cheered.

"Now it was my turn. I was asked to spell the word Mudita. Now, I knew how to spell Mudita. I had just learned the word from Dr. Ragland. but I said, Mudita, M-U-D-Y-T-A.

"The teacher who was calling out the words announced, sorry, that's incorrect. The word is spelled M-U-D-**I**-T-A. Bralyn is our winner.

"After the contest was over, Momma asked me why I spelled the word incorrectly. She knew I knew how to spell Mudita. I asked Momma if she knew what the word Mudita meant. She didn't understand.

"I told Momma that Mudita is a word that means I get great joy out of your joy and happiness out of your happiness.

"I told Momma, this is what I did. Bralyn is happy, she won. This makes me happy. So, in a way, I also won.

"Momma got this huge smile on her face. She laughed and told me she now understood. She told me that I was in love with Bralyn, and that made her happy. Then she said, Mudita.

"Bralyn never learned what I did, and that is what I wanted. Our friendship continued to grow throughout the year. And somewhere along the way she fell in love with me. Neither one of us knew what was happening. However, it happened.

"We started walking home from school together, then I asked Bralyn if she wanted to go to the

school dance with me.

"Little A, I didn't know how to dance, but that wasn't important. Bralyn said, yes. That was all that mattered.

"Bralyn was my first girlfriend. It was my first kiss. It was a kiss I will never forget. Little A, have you kissed a girl yet?

"No, Papa, no."

"Well, one day you will. You are a little young. However, when that time comes, you will know it. I don't think anyone ever forgets their first love, or their first kiss.

"Little A, It's past my bedtime. Good night young man, and Mudita."

Story # 20

A boy named Alec

Surprise, most kids actually like school, or they just like being away from mom and dad. I had a bad day at school today and was not in a good mood at bedtime. I told Papa all about my horrible day.

Then it was Papa's turn. He sat on the edge of his bed and told me a story I'll never forget. It was about school and friendship. It made me feel a lot better about school. School is a lot more than good grades. School is about everything.

Papa's story:

"Little A, you already know I liked school. It wasn't easy, but I knew it was important. And, surprisingly, I learned a lot during recess. I loved basketball. Plus, I learned to jump rope with the girls. Little A, can you jump rope? It's not easy, but it is fun.

"I learned to take turns and not make fun of other kids. I helped other kids when they needed help. I think I was a teacher long before becoming a teacher. I observed other students and learned from them.

"One day at recess I noticed a boy, about my age, who never played during recess. He was in a wheelchair, and just sat and watched us play. I don't know why, but no one played with him.

"So, one day, I went over and asked him if he wanted to play. He just looked at me and told me he couldn't walk. I told him that I could see that. I told him that I couldn't fly, and We both laughed. His name was Alec. We are still friends to this day, but he lives in California. He was white, blond hair, average size, but skinny legs, legs that required braces attached to his shoes.

"I told him he had a cool set of wheels, and that is how our friendship began. That first day we just talked. He told me a lot about himself. He just needed a friend, someone to talk to. The next day, at recess, I asked the school nurse to let me borrow the school wheelchair. When recess came, I rolled out the door in the wheelchair, and Alec started laughing. We shot baskets together and soon other boys joined us.

"My point is, Little A, school is a lot more than just Math and English. School is a place where you learn about people. They don't teach kindness in a classroom; They should, but they don't. You have to learn it on your own."

I told Papa that he was a good teacher and great friend. Papa taught me about life and about school and about treehouses.

Papa smiled and said, "Thank you, Little A. Now don't forget to say your prayers tonight, and MUDITA my young man, MUDITA."

Story # 21

Goodnight Papa

The next night Papa went to bed early. When I crawled into bed, I looked over at Papa. "Papa, tell me about your treehouse. Was it like the one we built? Who did you let into your treehouse? Was it as big as the one we built? Did you ever fall out of your treehouse, like I did?"

Papa was already asleep. In the morning Mom told me that Papa, over the night, had gone home to be with Jesus. She handed me a handwritten note from Papa. It was the start of another story. One day I will finish it. One day I will read it to my son while sitting in his treehouse.

Good night, Papa

                    The End

Postscript

Have you ever built a treehouse, out in the woods, away from everything and everyone?

Have you ever spent the night by yourself in a treehouse and listened to the night sounds; the sounds of someone or something moving around at the foot of the tree?

I had a rope ladder that extended from my treehouse down to the ground. I only let my best friends join me. And there were stories, lots of stories, great stories; stories that changed my life.

Only a person who has taught in the inner city schools is able to create a fictional, yet realistic account of the life of a youngster struggling to find himself in this environment.

John Chipley, whom the boys fondly have dubbed Mr. Chip, taught in Memphis inner-city schools for over fifteen years. In retirement he offers weekly volunteer sessions that focus on encouraging boys to read. This is a lofty goal, for the boys live in homes and neighborhood environments not structured to develop reading skills or dreams of career advancement. Mr. Chip's goal surpasses development of reading ability to encourage the boys to enjoy this privilege.

Chipley is formally prepared to teach, for he holds both Bachelor and Master of Education degrees. However, the most memorable aspect of his classroom presence is his heart. He cares deeply about each one of his students and is there for them both now and in the future. Through the persona of Little A, Chipley gives the boys a fictional character with whom they can identify. Little A's life style echoes theirs. While reading this series of books, the boys witness someone they can relate to. Little A is a wonderful fictional character full of wisdom, character, adventure, and confidence.

www.ingramcontent.com/pod-product-compliance
Lightning Source LLC
LaVergne TN
LVHW022000060526
838201LV00048B/1640